**At the Court of Queen Elizabeth**

# Tartan Means Trouble

## by Karen Wallace

### Illustrated by Jane Cope

# W
# FRANKLIN WATTS
## LONDON•SYDNEY

First published in 2001 by
Franklin Watts
96 Leonard Street
London EC2A 4XD

Franklin Watts Australia
56 O'Riordan Street
Alexandria
NSW 2015

Editor: Louise John
Designer: Jason Anscomb
Consultant: Dr Anne Millard, BA Hons, Dip Ed, PhD

A CIP catalogue record for this book
is available from the British Library.

ISBN    0 7496 4072 3 (hbk)
        0 7496 4372 2 (pbk)

Dewey Classification 942.05

Printed in Great Britain

At the Court of Queen Elizabeth

# Tartan Means Trouble

by Karen Wallace

Illustrated by Jane Cope

**W**
FRANKLIN WATTS
LONDON • SYDNEY

# The Characters

Mary Marchbank

Old Ma Knucklebone

Matilda, Lady Mouthwater

Queen Elizabeth

Toby Crumble

Earl Inkblot

Mary Queen of Scots

Sydney Woodshavings

# CONTENTS

## CHAPTER ONE
### A Queen's Promise

Mary Marchbank, lady's maid to Queen Elizabeth I, sat down on a bench in the royal herb garden and tied up a big bunch of marjoram with a piece of red ribbon.

Marjoram was the Queen's favourite herb. The smell of it soothed her temper, so her maids always picked lots.

The Queen's herb garden looked like a miniature maze. Tiny clipped hedges twisted and turned around beds of herbs and flowers. Between the hedges, winding paths were covered with different coloured gravel. Today it was sunny and the paths glittered as if they were sprinkled with jewels.

Mary leaned back and breathed in deeply. The garden was full of the sound of buzzing bees and the smell of lavender. Mary loved lavender. And now, at last, she had a reason to pick it.

She pushed aside the marjoram in her basket. Then she walked down the path and began to pull up spike after spike of sticky blue lavender.

In her mind's eye Mary saw herself hanging the lavender up to dry, then sewing the crumbly blue flowers into tiny muslin sachets.

She saw herself putting the sweet smelling sachets into a wooden chest full of sheets, pillow cases, napkins and tablecloths – all the precious linen she had put aside for her wedding day.

A huge smile spread across Mary's face as she remembered the note her sweetheart, Sydney Woodshavings, had sent her last week:

*Meet me in the herb garden. I have tender tidings for us both.*

Sydney had been waiting when Mary ran into the garden. She had sat beside him on the bench and they held hands as he spoke.

"Our mistress has agreed to let us marry, dear!" Sydney had whispered. "In the autumn, she said, when the stags run in the woods and she is busy with hunting."

And Mary's heart had thumped so loudly in her chest that she was sure her dear Sydney would hear it!

Now, as Mary tied up her lavender and picked one last bunch of marjoram, she thought of all the things she had to do over the next two months.

The Queen was not the only one who would be busy!

***

Sitting in her usual place in the Queen's chamber – that is to say, as far away from the Queen's special chair as possible – Matilda, Lady Mouthwater was sketching the outline of the new tapestry she was about to begin.

It was a picture of rolling hills with the sea sparkling in the distance.

A coach was making its way along a winding road. Inside the coach was a woman who looked distinctly like Matilda, Lady Mouthwater.

The woman looked as if she had come a long way. And, if the amount of trunks and boxes tied to the coach roof were anything to go by, she looked as if she was not intending to return.

A strange look flickered over Matilda, Lady Mouthwater's long lizardy face. It was almost as if she was smiling.

And indeed that was exactly what Matilda, Lady Mouthwater was doing!

Because at long last the Queen had given her permission to go back home to her mother in Devon. "You may leave when the stags run in the woods," the Queen had said. "I shall be busy then and will not need your services."

At the time, Matilda, Lady Mouthwater had almost fainted! For years now she had been asking the Queen's permission to leave the court.

And for years and years the Queen had refused. It was almost as if the Queen enjoyed watching her lady-in-waiting suffer.

Poor Matilda, Lady Mouthwater! She had been made to play horrible games of cards she wasn't allowed to win. She had been forced into bathtubs of icy water to play battle games with toy ships. She had even been led blindfolded into one of the Queen's mazes and left there overnight.

But that hadn't been a real game.

The Queen had done it just for fun!

Matilda, Lady Mouthwater, sighed and looked down at her picture. The tapestry would be ready to present to the Queen in two months.

After that, Matilda, Lady Mouthwater would be gone in a cloud of dust and coach wheels.

\*\*\*

Godfrey, Earl Inkblot, sat behind his great oak table. He was staring at a map of the world. A half-carved wooden ship was in his hands.

It was a funny looking little ship because Godfrey, Earl Inkblot wasn't much good at carving. And besides, his hands shook so much nowadays, he could barely get his food to his mouth.

Godfrey, Earl Inkblot, sighed and remembered the time when he had been at university. He had spent his days studying and his nights staring at maps of the world.

He had sworn to himself that he would visit these faraway places while he was young and strong. Then something had happened that had changed his life completely.

Godfrey, Earl Inkblot, was summoned to serve the Queen.

And soon the only map he remembered was the quickest route out of the Queen's palace!

Godfrey, Earl Inkblot, pulled a face. Or perhaps it was a smile? It was hard to tell these days.

Force of habit made him look over his shoulder to see if someone was watching him – someone with thin, red hair and a mean glint in her eye.

Godfrey, Earl Inkblot heaved a huge sigh of relief. He was alone!

Earl Inkblot held up the little ship and stared at it. On the front, he had carved a tiny figure. It had a bushy beard and a blotchy face just like him! Then he made a peculiar whooshing noise as he pushed the ship across the blue bits of the map.

It was as if Godfrey, Earl Inkblot was pretending he was sailing across the ocean.

And that's exactly what he was doing. Because finally, after years and years of asking, the Queen had given him permission to retire from her court.

"You may leave when the stags run in the woods," she had said. "I shall be busy then and will not need your services."

Godfrey, Earl
Inkblot, picked up his
penknife and began
to carve the curl of a
wave against the side
of his ship.

It would be ready
to present to the
Queen in two
months.

After that,
he'd be off to sea
faster than a rat
up the rigging!

Down in the great kitchen of the Queen's palace, Toby Crumble couldn't believe his good fortune and was actually humming a happy tune! He pulled out a shallow oval dish and began to fill it with sliced apples. Then he rubbed some flour and butter together until it was nice and crumbly. He sprinkled this over the apples, covered them with brown sugar and dusted them with cinnamon.

This pudding was the Queen's favourite and Toby had invented it himself. For years and years he had made it for the Queen whenever she wanted it, including in the middle of the night!

And for years and years, Toby had humbly been requesting permission to call his pudding Apple Crumble.

After all that's what happened to the flour and butter when you rubbed them together – they crumbled, and Crumble was his name too!

A warm flush of pleasure spread across Toby's chubby face. Last week, out of the blue, the Queen had suddenly said agreed!

Toby picked up the shallow dish and put it in the oven.

Apple Crumble was here to stay!

## CHAPTER TWO
### A Nasty Letter

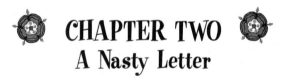

Mary Queen of Scots peered at herself in a looking glass. There was no doubt about it. She was much more beautiful than her cousin Elizabeth, the Queen of England.

Her eyes were a dark, glossy brown while the Queen's were said to be a watery green. Mary's long hair was thick and shiny while the Queen's was said to be thin and carroty-coloured.

Mary pulled back her lips and practised a ravishing smile. Even her teeth were better. There were more of them for a start!

In fact, there was only one way in which her blasted cousin was better than her – Queen Elizabeth I had more power!

Mary smashed the looking glass on the floor. She desperately wanted to go back to Scotland but the Queen wouldn't let her.

And it was because of that cursed power that Mary was stuck in the north of England in a cold damp house with an English Lord, his filthy food and his ugly gossiping wife!

Mary Queen of Scots stomped across the polished oak floor and pulled open a chest. She knelt down and began throwing clothes onto the floor.

Finally, she found what she was looking for.

It was a piece of tartan cloth, dyed red and orange, black and purple. Woven together, the colours looked like a cross between a bruise and a bad case of sunburn.

A nasty grin spread across Mary's face. She sat down in the chair in front of her writing table and pulled a piece of paper towards her.

"I'll show that red-headed bully," she muttered. "I'll make so much trouble, she'll be only too glad to be rid of me!"

And with that, Mary Queen of Scots dipped her quill pen in a pot of black ink and began to write...

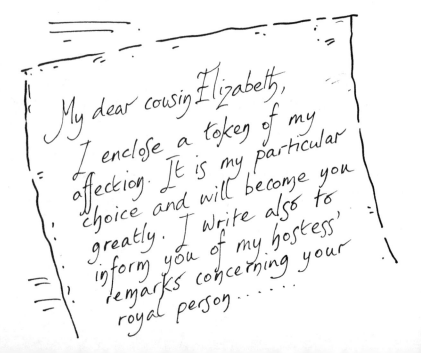

My dear cousin Elizabeth,
I enclose a token of my affection. It is my particular choice and will become you greatly. I write also to inform you of my hostess' remarks concerning your royal person......

\*\*\*

Mary Marchbank sighed and looked down at the seal on the parcel addressed to the Queen.

It was the seal of Mary Queen of Scots. And everything to do with Mary Queen of Scots meant trouble these days.

Not only was she trying to go back to Scotland again, even after she had been driven out by her own people, but some said she also had eyes for the throne of England!

And, as well as what was going on between the two countries, Mary knew there was no love lost between the two cousins, either.

Indeed, whenever her cousin's name was mentioned, the Queen went a nasty purplish, red colour.

Mary picked up the parcel and her heart sank.

There was only a week to go before the hunting season began. And that meant there was only a week before she was to marry Sydney and move into the little cottage he had built for her!

Mary crossed her fingers and hoped against hope that everything would go smoothly.
At that moment, Godfrey, Earl Inkblot skipped down the corridor.

Ever since the Queen had given him permission to leave the court, Godfrey, Earl Inkblot had been so happy, he had been skipping everywhere.

Now he couldn't help doing a tiny twirl in the air.

There was only one week to go until he left the Queen's court and his sea bag was packed and ready!

"Good morning, Mary!" cried Earl Inkblot.
He smiled broadly and tickled Mary under the chin.
"Why the long face?"

"I must deliver this parcel to my mistress,"
explained Mary. "It's from –"

"Tush, child!" grinned the Earl of Inkblot. "'Tis
only a parcel." He held out his hand. "Here, give it
to me!"

At that moment, the smell of hot sweet apples
wafted down the corridor. Toby Crumble walked
towards them, holding an oval dish in his hands.

**HOME SWEET HOME IN ELIZABETHAN TIMES**

"Apple Crumble!" he said proudly, holding up the dish. "Her Majesty has demanded some for her breakfast."

"Then we shall greet her bearing gifts," cried Earl Inkblot in a high joyful voice, waving the parcel, "and wish her well on this glorious morning."

\*\*\*

Queen Elizabeth I of England stood with her feet apart in the middle of her chamber.

Her jaw was set like a hatchet and her face was as black as the thunder cloud that had just blocked out the sun behind her.

Rain drops started to pitter patter on the glass.

Mary Marchbank stood behind Matilda, Lady

Mouthwater and Godfrey, Earl Inkblot.

From the moment the Queen had ripped open her parcel, Mary's stomach had felt as if it was full of snow. And now that snow was turning to hard lumps of ice.

In one hand, the Queen held a letter. In the other, she held a piece of woollen cloth. It was a strange-looking mixture of red, orange, purple and black.

But the strangest thing of all was that somehow it exactly matched the Queen's face!

"How dare my cousin suggest this disgusting colour becomes me!" screeched the Queen.

SMASH! A dainty china plate hit the wall.

"It is the colour of a bruise!"

"But, Your Majesty – " murmured Earl Inkblot as gently as he could.

"Shaddup!" bellowed the Queen. She snapped open the letter again.

"She says I am called a sickly scarecrow! She says my courtiers tell flattering lies to win my favour!"

As the Queen spoke, her voice grew higher and higher and louder and louder.

"But Madam," protested Matilda, Lady Mouthwater in the most soothing voice she could manage.

"Shaddup!" yelled the Queen. She turned back to the letter. "I am reported to be as bald as a coot and as wrinkled as a prune!"

The Queen kicked over a table and thrust her purple face forwards.

"IS IT TRUE?" she screamed at Godfrey, Earl Inkblot.

"IS IT TRUE?" she screeched at Matilda, Lady Mouthwater.

Earl Inkblot made a sound like a camel choking. Matilda, Lady Mouthwater opened her mouth but no noise came out. Toby Crumble was so frightened, he hid under a chair.

Mary Marchbank stepped forward. At times like these, the soothing smell of marjoram always did the trick. She held out a jug of steaming water. A large bunch of marjoram floated on the top.

"Of course, it's not true, Your Majesty," said Mary, gently.

The Queen spun round.

Her eyeballs were as red as the cloth in her hand. Her mouth was a black line woven across her purple face.

"LIAR!" she screeched.

# CHAPTER THREE
## Love at First Sight

Mary Marchbank had never seen a grown man cry. Even Sydney Woodshavings, when she told him that the Queen had changed her mind and wouldn't be hunting this season, had but stamped on the floor and turned back to his hammering.

Now Godfrey, Earl Inkblot sat slumped in the corner of the room. He wiped his nose on his embroidered velvet sleeve and sniffed.

"But she promised!" he wailed. "I packed my sea bag and everything!"

Mary held out a large white handkerchief. It was the second one she had handed out that morning. The first had been to Matilda, Lady Mouthwater, who Mary had found sitting miserably in her chair sketching out a new tapestry.

The tapestry looked like something out of a horror story. A fairy queen was being ripped apart by a dragon and gobbled up by a giant.

Even poor Toby Crumble was inconsolable.

The Queen had thrown his Apple Crumble on the floor and vowed never to eat one again.

Mary fought back an urge to pat Earl Inkblot on the shoulder.

"Don't you worry, my lord," said Mary kindly. "The Queen is always changing her mind. Perhaps we can make her think again."

Godfrey, Earl Inkblot hooted into the large white handkerchief. "But how?" he yowled. "That pesky Queen of Scots wants to make as much trouble as she can!"

He sighed and rubbed his red eyes. "It's hopeless. We'll all be stuck here for ever."

Mary pulled a face. That was exactly what Matilda, Lady Mouthwater had said.

"It's not hopeless," she said firmly. "There must be a way, or someone we could ask for help."

"We need some kind of spell more like," muttered Godfrey, Earl Inkblot. "That Scottish Queen is more cunning than a pack of foxes."

Suddenly, Mary had a brilliant idea. There *was* someone they could talk to!

Someone who was a cunning old fox herself. Old Ma Knucklebone, of course!

For the first time since the Queen had opened the terrible parcel, Mary felt the tiniest bubble of hope rise inside her. Why hadn't she thought of Old Ma Knucklebone before? She even wore a lucky foxtail pinned to the back of her cap.

"Sir," said Mary quietly. "Would you consent to visit a cunning old fox who could help us?"

"Consent?" cried Godfrey, Earl Inkblot. "Why, I'll do anything!"

\*\*\*

And that was how Godfrey, the Earl of Inkblot, found himself, disguised in a ragged cloak, walking down a narrow street towards Old Ma Knucklebone's hovel.

Mary had given him precise instructions. First right past the butcher's guts bucket. Second left past the fat boiler's house.

Then she had stared at her feet and blushed.

"I'd say the smell will tell you when you have arrived at the right place, my lord."

Now Godfrey pushed past a butcher's stall that was half hidden behind a cloud of flies. He reached into his ragged pocket and pulled out a scented handkerchief to press to his nose. It was the only way he could stop himself being sick.

Sure enough, on one side of the butcher's stall, was a huge wooden bucket full of guts. Earl Inkblot ran down the first narrow street and turned left in front of a man in a red felt hat, stirring a cauldron of fat. He wafted the greasy black smoke away.

"I seek the widow Knucklebone!" he shouted.

The man grinned a toothless grin and pointed across the way to a dirty, red door.

Earl Inkblot bowed. He was just about to tip the man a farthing when he remembered he was supposed to be a peddler. Then he crossed the muddy street and banged on the door.

\*\*\*

Old Ma Knucklebone stared at the bearded man with the blotchy face who sat nervously in her kitchen.

He had taken off his peddler's cloak. Then he had asked humbly and courteously for her help.

As Old Ma Knucklebone had listened, she had absent-mindedly stuck a thick finger into a gluey potion and popped it in her mouth. It was a love potion – one taste and you fall hopelessly in love with the first person you see.

Old Ma Knucklebone stared deep into Earl Inkblot's red-rimmed eyes.

A warm feeling surged from the ends of her lumpy toes to the top of her greasy head. And she knew, as she rolled her famous bones across the table, that this time she would read the message for free!

Indeed, she would do anything for Godfrey, Earl Inkblot!  Because Old Ma Knucklebone was in love!

## CHAPTER FOUR
### Trick or Traitor?

Mary Marchbank's face was whiter than a newly-washed linen sheet. For the first time in her life, she had no idea what she should do.

In front of her the Queen was sitting in the middle of the floor jabbing pins into a doll that looked remarkably like Mary Queen of Scots.

Beside her, slumped in a chair was Matilda, Lady Mouthwater. Her dress was soaking wet and a bunch of marjoram sat on her head, drooping down over her face. A broken jug lay in pieces on the floor.

Poor Matilda, Lady Mouthwater! It had been her job that morning to read out the Queen's letters.

At the beginning everything seemed to be going well. There were poems praising the Queen's beauty from courtiers all over the country. There were letters from French Princes sending presents and asking for the Queen's hand in marriage.

And then, tucked in amongst them, was a letter from Mary Queen of Scots. Matilda, Lady Mouthwater had already started to read it before she realised and by then it was too late to stop.

Mary Marchbank bit her lip as she remembered poor Lady Mouthwater's trembling voice.

According to Mary Queen of Scots, it was said Queen Elizabeth's teeth were as black as lumps of coal and her eyes were as watery as a swamp. It was known she had a temper like a bull and clouted her servants. It was reported she was an old lady who chased young courtiers round her palace, demanding that they pay her compliments.

Then there had been a terrible SMASH as the jug of marjoram water had landed on Lady Mouthwater's head.

"I hate her! I hate her! I hate her!" screamed the Queen. She picked up the doll and ripped off its head. "How dare my cousin torment me so?"

Mary begin to pick up the scattered pieces of broken china. Carefully, she pulled back one of Matilda, Lady Mouthwater's, eyelids. She was still out for the count!

"If it pleases, Your Majesty," whispered Mary. "There may be a way to stop these letters."

"How?" The Queen sniffed. And for the first time, Mary saw that she was as upset as she was angry. Because the truth hurt – her teeth *were* black and her eyes *were* watery. She was getting old.

"The Queen of Scots couldn't write such letters if she was in a more secure house," said Godfrey Earl Inkblot, stepping into the Queen's chamber.

Mary spun round. After the Earl's secret visit, she knew that whatever he suggested would be straight from Old Ma Knucklebone's lips.

"You mean a prison?" snapped the Queen. "How can we do that? She is no traitor."

"Not yet," replied Earl Inkblot slowly. "But if we sent certain letters from say –" he swallowed nervously. "A made-up secret admirer who wanted to see her crowned Queen of England?"

"What treasonable rogue would want such a thing?" yelled the Queen. She grabbed the bedpost and flung herself up on the bed. "I shall have him in thumb screws and stretched on the rack!"

"Would be but a trick, Your Majesty," said the Earl Inkblot as quickly as he could. "A cunning trick to trap the Queen of Scots so that she may not write you any more nasty letters."

The Queen chewed her lip thoughtfully. "Ah, yes, a trick," she said slowly. "I see what you mean."

She climbed off her bed and looked over to where Matilda, Lady Mouthwater was still slumped. For a moment, she looked almost sorry.

"Do what you will, Earl Inkblot," muttered the Queen. "My cousin's words are unkind and irksome and I find I am provoked to do strange things."

Then she flicked off the bunch of wet marjoram that sat on top of Matilda, Lady Mouthwater's head and swept out of the room.

# CRIME AND PUNISHMENT TUDOR STYLE

The prisoner gets branded.

The prisoner gets stretched on the rack.

The prisoner gets her hands chopped off.

"It's all very well promising to write a letter," muttered Godfrey, Earl of Inkblot. "But I don't have the faintest notion of what to say or where to begin."

"But this was all your idea," snapped Matilda, Lady Mouthwater.

Ever since the incident with the jug of marjoram water, poor Lady Mouthwater was inclined to be rather edgy.

"It was Old Ma Knucklebone who suggested it, my lady," murmured Mary, gently.

"Then she should write it," snarled Matilda, Lady Mouthwater.

At that moment, something huffed and puffed and scratched at the door. It sounded like a huge rat.

"Who's that?" cried Godfrey, Earl Inkblot, leaping nervously out of his chair.

The door opened and a truly terrible smell filled the room. It was a strange combination of pigsty and rosewater.

"Old Ma Knucklebone come to pay her respects, lords and ladies."

Mary Marchbank gasped.

Old Ma Knucklebone's filthy grey dress was decorated with pink ribbons. Red roses had been embroidered on her dirty apron.

But strangest of all, a small red satin heart had been pinned to the lucky foxtail that hung from her greasy cap.

"I had this letter written specially for you, Sir Godfrey," simpered Old Ma Knucklebone. She curtseyed and held out a rolled parchment. It was sealed with a tiny blob of wax.

Godfrey, Earl Inkblot took the roll and stared down at the seal.

Old Ma Knucklebone seemed to hold her breath. "'Tis best broken with your teeth," she said in a breathy voice.

Then she watched with glistening lips as

Godfrey, Earl Inkblot, lifted the rolled parchment to his lips and sank his teeth into the wax.

He didn't notice the tiny blob of gluey love potion that was hidden underneath.

All he knew was that, when he looked up again, he found himself staring deep into Old Ma Knucklebone's bright squirrelly eyes. A warm feeling rose from the end of his long, skinny toes to the top of his big, curly-haired head.

Godfrey, Earl Inkblot was in love!

# CHAPTER FIVE
## A Cunning Trap

Mary Queen of Scots picked up the letter and read it for a second time.

*Most glorious Queen, your beauty is a star shining bright in the sky. For that reason alone, you are Queen of the Universe. Your wit and your wisdom are twin towers stretching up to the heavens. For that reason alone, you should be Queen of this Land.*

*Only say yes, and I, your most devoted admirer,
along with my fellow devoted admirers, will rescue you
from your damp, dark house and place you on the
throne of England where you belong!*

   *Yours aye,*

      *Gilbert, Ink of Earlblot*


*P.S. To out-fox your ugly cousin's cunning spies, wrap
this letter in greased paper and bury it in a flower pot
on the window ledge.*


Mary Queen of Scots twirled around the room
and kissed her reflection
in the looking glass.

At last, after all her
plotting and planning,
her time had come!

At last she would
be Queen of England!
She closed her eyes
and imagined herself
sitting on the throne,
dressed from head to
toe in cloth of gold.

MARY QUEEN OF SCOTS – DARK, DEVIOUS AND DETERMINED TO STEAL ELIZABETH'S CROWN
I'm prettier than her too.

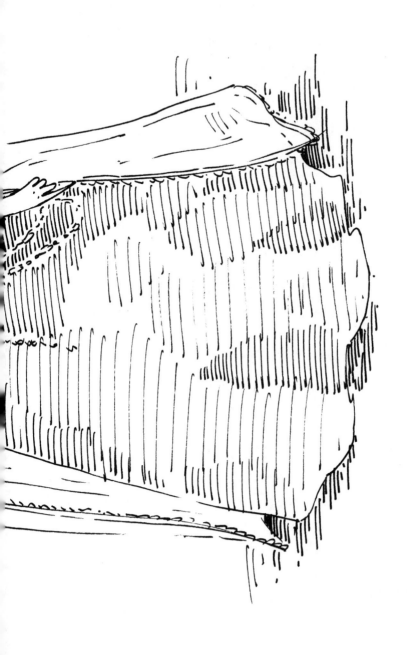

She made a fist and punched the air.

"Yessss!" she shouted.

Mary Queen of Scots sat down at her desk, pulled out a piece of paper and began to write.

*My dear Ink of Earlblot,*
*You have made a lonely Queen very happy...*

\*\*\*

Mary Marchbank looked down at the letter that had just arrived by messenger from the north of England.

It was addressed to Gilbert, Ink of Earlblot! Mary's heart leapt in her chest! The Ink of Earlblot had been Old Ma Knucklebone's clever idea.

Now they knew that the Queen of Scots had taken the bait and agreed to plot against Queen

Elizabeth. And plotting against the Queen was a very serious business, indeed.

Mary took a deep breath. She hoped against hope that this letter was the proof they needed to stop the Queen of Scots in her tracks.

At that moment, Godfrey, Earl Inkblot, skipped down the corridor.

It was amazing!

Even though the Queen had refused him permission to leave the court, from the moment he had broken the seal on Old Ma Knucklebone's letter, Earl Inkblot spent his days humming and skipping or staring dreamily out of the window.

"Good morning, Mary!" cried Earl Inkblot. "And what a wonderful day it is, too!"

Mary showed him the letter. "I hope it stays that way," she murmured.

A smell of hot sweet apples wafted down the corridor. Toby Crumble walked quickly towards them. He held a shallow, oval dish in his hand.

"Toby!" cried Mary in a puzzled voice. "I thought –"

Toby grinned nervously. "Old Ma Knucklebone said I was to take the Queen my pudding at the same time as you took her the letter."

"But how did you know the letter would arrive today?" cried Mary.

Toby shrugged. "Old Ma Knucklebone said it would."

Mary couldn't believe it. It was almost as if Old Ma Knucklebone had put them all under some kind of spell.

She turned and looked at Earl Inkblot. He was humming a little tune and staring dreamily out of the window.

"I just hope the spell works," muttered Mary to herself as they came to the door of the Queen's chamber.

# 🌸 CHAPTER SIX 🌸
## Some Dreams Come True

Queen Elizabeth I of England sat at her desk in the middle of her chamber.

The letter from Mary Queen of Scots to Gilbert, Ink of Earlblot was in front of her.

On the other side of the room, near the door, stood Godfrey, Earl Inkblot.

Matilda, Lady Mouthwater preferred to be nearer to the window. She knew it was more dangerous to jump than to run, but you could get away quicker.

Mary Marchbank reached for a bunch of marjoram and held it nervously behind her back.

As for Toby Crumble, even though Old Ma Knucklebone had told him he had nothing to worry about, he waited outside in the corridor anyway. It was bad enough getting a jug of water over your head, but a dish of hot Apple Crumble would not be funny at all.

Inside the Queen's chamber nobody spoke. Indeed, you could have heard a mouse cough.

At last the Queen looked up from the letter. "Treason is a very serious matter," said the Queen in a low voice. "The Queen of Scots has been very, very foolish."

Again nobody spoke.

"But you have all been very, very clever," said the Queen. She laughed gaily. "Gilbert, Ink of Earlblot – I like that!"

Then the Queen stood up, took a deep breath and shouted as loud as she could. "BECAUSE NOW I CAN SEND THE STUPID OLD COW TO JAIL!"

The Queen picked up the piece of tartan cloth that Mary had sent to her earlier.

"And as for this rag! Give it to the first old witch you see!"

And she chucked it across the room.

Godfrey, Earl Inkblot watched as the purples and reds and oranges and blacks of the tartan swirled past him.

Suddenly his face went all gooey.

The cloth would look lovely around Old Ma Knucklebone's shoulders! They were just her colours, too! He grabbed the cloth and ran out the door.

The Queen threw back her head and laughed. "Strewth!" she cried. "Why, anyone would think that man was in love."

*** 

Old Ma Knucklebone chuckled to herself as she stared at the grimy bones that lay on her table. The bones always told her everything.

She could see Mary Marchbank sitting with Sydney Woodshavings in the Queen's herb garden. The Queen had given Mary the afternoon off. One day Mary would marry her sweetheart, but not yet!

And there was Matilda, Lady Mouthwater, climbing into a country coach! The Queen had agreed to let her pay a visit to her mother. And after all, a few days was better than nothing.

Old Ma Knucklebone smiled. She could even see the Queen tucking into a big dish of Apple Crumble. It didn't matter if she was old and toothless, there would be no more letters from her cousin to tell her so.

Finally, Old Ma Knucklebone saw a bearded blotchy-faced man hurrying down the street, carrying a particularly pretty piece of material. It was red, purple, black and orange – all her favourite colours!

Old Ma Knucklebone grinned and tipped a bottle of rosewater over herself.

Queens and their courts may come and go but the bones never lie!

# ❀ NOTES ❀
## At the Court of Queen Elizabeth
### (How it really was!)

### Mary Queen of Scots

Mary Queen of Scots was Queen Elizabeth's cousin. She was also a Catholic, which meant that powerful Catholics in England and Europe wanted to assassinate Elizabeth and put Mary on the throne.

Mary was kept prisoner in England for many years under suspicion of plotting to overthrow the Queen. Finally, the Queen's spies obtained proof of these accusations and Mary was beheaded in 1587.

### Tudor Gardens

Elizabethans were keen gardeners. They grew all sorts of vegetables and fruit, including exotic varieties like white peaches and apricots. They were particularly fond of ornamental gardens, laid out with formal flower beds and separated by beautifully clipped hedges.

## Elizabethan Buildings

There was a building boom during the Elizabethan period. For the first time, people from all levels of society started to build houses that were more than protection from the weather and defence from enemies.

Most Elizabethans favoured timber-framed buildings, which could be made big or small, elaborate or simple. The timbers were made of oak and many of them are still lived in today.

## Crime and Punishment

Punishments were harsh for those convicted of plotting against the State. The victim was invariably tortured to get a full confession. One method of torture was the rack, where the victim's body was stretched until his or her joints were dislocated.

High-ranking traitors like Mary Queen of Scots were beheaded. The executioner was often paid to sharpen his axe first, so it would make a clean cut!

Common traitors were hanged, drawn and quartered. This means that their bodies were cut down and their insides were scraped out before they were dead.

## Tartans

Tartan was a tightly woven woollen material, worn primarily by Highlanders in Scotland. Originally the material was cut into a long piece called a 'plaid' and worn over the shoulder and across the chest.

Later 'plaid' became the word to describe the actual cloth. It wasn't until much later on that each Highland Clan had its own plaid or tartan.